X
y
z

The Child's World®

Published in the United States of America by The Child's World®
1980 Lookout Drive • Mankato, MN 56003-1705
800-599-READ • www.childsworld.com

ACKNOWLEDGMENTS
The Child's World®: Mary Berendes, Publishing Director
The Design Lab: Kathleen Petelinsek, Design and Page Production
Literacy Consultants: Cecilia Minden, PhD, and Joanne Meier, PhD

LIBRARY OF CONGRESS
CATALOGING-IN-PUBLICATION DATA
Moncure, Jane Belk.
  My "xyz" sound box / by Jane Belk Moncure;
illustrated by Rebecca Thornburgh.
     p. cm. — (Sound box books)
  Summary: "Little x, y, and z all have adventures with items begin-
ning with their respective letter's sound, such as x-rays, yellow
yo-yos, and zippy zebras at the zoo."—Provided by publisher.
  ISBN 978-1-60253-164-2 (library bound : alk. paper)
  [1. Alphabet.] I. Thornburgh, Rebecca McKillip, ill. II. Title.
III. Series.
  PZ7.M739Myx 2009
  [E]–dc22   2008033154

A NOTE TO PARENTS AND EDUCATORS:

Magic moon machines and five fat frogs are just a few of the fun things you can share with children by reading books with them. Reading aloud helps children in so many ways! It introduces them to new words, motivates them to develop their own reading skills, and expands their attention span and listening abilities. So it's important to find time each day to share a book or two . . . or three!

As you read with young children, you can help develop their understanding of how print works by talking about the parts of the book—the cover, the title, the illustrations, and the words that tell the story. As you read, use your finger to point to each word, modeling a gentle sweep from left to right.

Simple word games help develop important prereading skills, including an understanding of rhyme and alliteration (when words share the same beginning sound, such as "six" and "sand"). Try playing with words from a book you've just shared: "What other words start with the same sound as moon?" "Cat and hat, do those words rhyme?" The possibilities are endless—and so are the rewards!

My "x y z" Sound Box®

X
Y
Z

WRITTEN BY JANE BELK MONCURE

ILLUSTRATED BY REBECCA THORNBURGH

Little  had a box. "I will find

things that begin with my letter,"

he said. "I will put them into my

sound box."

Little  found an x-ray machine.

"Excellent," said Little 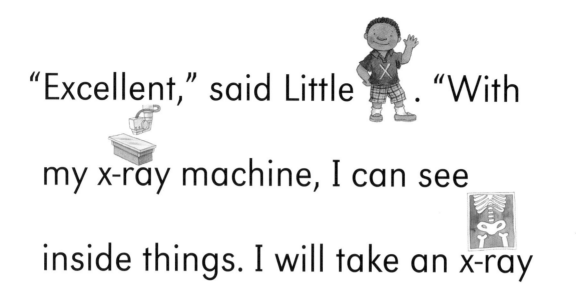. "With my x-ray machine, I can see inside things. I will take an x-ray of my hands."

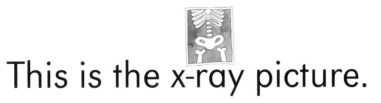
This is the x-ray picture.

"Excellent," he said.

"The x-ray shows the bones in my  hands." He put the x-ray picture into his sound box.

"I will take an x-ray of my feet,"

he said. This is the x-ray picture.

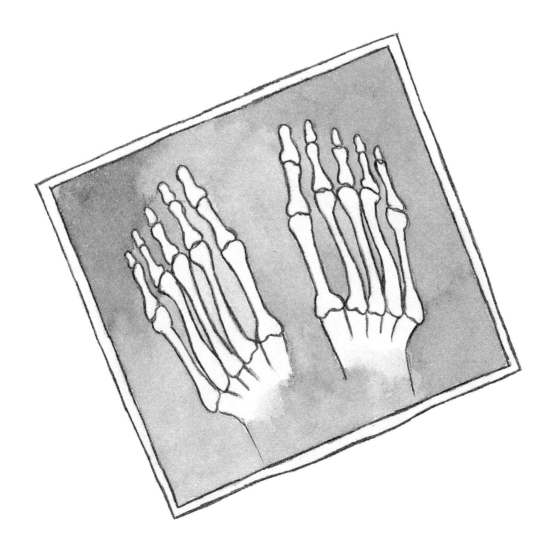

"Excellent," said Little . "The x-ray shows the bones in my feet."

Then he put the x-ray picture

and the x-ray machine into his

sound box.

He said, "Now I will call my friend, Little . I will see if he  has a sound box."

"I do," said Little . "I will find

something that begins with my

 sound. I will put it into my

sound box."

Little  found a yo-yo. It was

a yellow yo-yo. He tried to make

the yo-yo go down and up.

But the string was too short.

Little 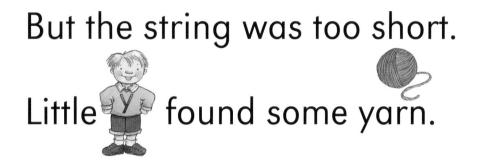 found some yarn.

He tied it to the string.

Now the yo-yo went way-y-y

down and way-y-y up, way-y-y

down and way-y-y up.

Little  turned his box upside
down. He stood on his box with
the yo-yo.

He said, "Now I will call my friend Little  and see if she has a sound box."

"I do," said Little . "I will find

things that begin with my

sound. I will put them into my

sound box."

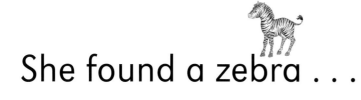

She found a zebra . . .

and another zebra, and

another zebra.

Little 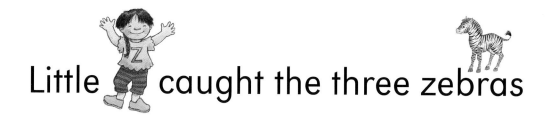 caught the three zebras

and . . .

tried to put them into the box.

But the zebras jumped out of

the box! Zip! Zip! Zip!

They ran zigzag down the road.

"I will catch you, zippy zebras!"

cried Little Z. And she did.

Then she took the zebras to
the zoo.

Little , and 's Word List

x-ray machine

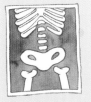

x-ray picture

yarn

yo-yo

zebra

zoo

Other Words with Little 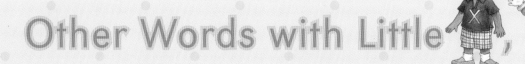, and

Xerox® machine

xylophone

yacht

yak

yam

yardstick

zero

zinnia

zipper

zucchini

More to Do!

You can get extra practice with letters by using yarn to make some zippy letters! Here's what you'll need to make a fun set of alphabet cards:

What you need:
- index cards
- a pencil
- glue
- yarn

Directions:

1. With your pencil, write a large letter on each index card.

2. Trace over your pencil mark with a thin line of glue.

3. Lay some yarn on top of the glue. Cut any leftover yarn at the end. Carefully press down on the yarn piece to help it dry in place.

4. After the cards are dry, gently trace over each letter with your finger.

5. Now you can play lots of games! Put your alphabet cards in order. Spell out simple words like x-ray, yarn, yam, zip, and zap!

About the Author

Best-selling author Jane Belk Moncure has written over 300 books throughout her teaching and writing career. After earning a Master's degree in Early Childhood Education from Columbia University, she became one of the pioneers in that field. In 1956, she helped form the Virginia Association for Early Childhood Education, which established the first statewide standards for teachers of young children.

Inspired by her work in the classroom, Mrs. Moncure's books have become standards in primary education, and her name is recognized across the country. Her success is reflected not only in her books' popularity with parents, children, and educators, but also by numerous awards, including the 1984 C. S. Lewis Gold Medal Award.

About the Illustrator

Rebecca Thornburgh lives in a pleasantly spooky old house in Philadelphia. If she's not at her drawing table, she's reading—or singing with her band, called Reckless Amateurs. Rebecca has one husband, two daughters, and two silly dogs.